Shoo Rayner began his career as an illustrator in a garden shed near Machynlleth. He drew for Michael Morpurgo and Rose Impey, but editors kept encouraging him to write. Over 200 books later, Shoo, well known for his many fast-paced series for newly confident readers, has been building a worldwide following for his award winning how-to-draw videos on YouTube. Shoo lives in the Forest of Dean with his wife and their cat.

www.shoorayner.com

Also by Shoo Rayner
from Firefly Press:

Walker
And the Dragon Series:
Dragon Gold
Dragon White
Dragon Red

WALKER

THE MYSTERY OF THE
MISSING MILLIONS

Firefly

First published in 2021
by Firefly Press
25 Gabalfa Road, Llandaff North,
Cardiff, CF14 2JJ
www.fireflypress.co.uk

A CIP catalogue record of this book is available
from the British Library.

1 3 5 7 9 8 6 4 2

print ISBN 9781913102531
ebook ISBN 9781913102548

*This book has been published with the support of
the Books Council Wales.*

Typeset by Elaine Sharples

Printed and bound by CPI Group UK

For Abigail
A dog person, if ever there was one!

Welcome to Foxley!

This is Walker.
He can't have a dog because his mother is allergic,
so he walks other people's dogs in his village.

He walks Stella. Her owner is Jenny.

He used to walk Loki and Thor for
Arlington Wherewithal (until he caught Arlington
running a puppy farm and got him arrested!)
This is Arlington's wife,
Jazzaminta, and her dog, Camilla:

This is Walker's best friend, Anje, and her dog, Boss. This is her dad, Mr Bonus, who runs the village shop.

Here are the local police, Dectective Inspector Triggs, Constable Krish Malik, and police dog Raffi.

And who are the people spying on everyone with their dog, Bolt? You'll have to read to find out...

'Walker!' Dad called upstairs from the front door. 'It's the police! They want to talk to you!'

Walker felt his stomach lurch, as if he was racing downhill on a rollercoaster. The police! What did they want? Warily, he descended the stairs into the hall.

'This is Constable Malik,' said Dad, looking concerned. 'He wants a word with you.'

The police officer's silhouette blocked the doorway. His protective vest bristled with camera and radio equipment. Walker's eyes were drawn to the handcuffs on his belt. Was he going to be arrested? What had he done wrong?

'Call me Krish.' The police officer smiled. 'And this is Raffi.' Krish tugged a leash by his side. A German shepherd sidled out from behind him.

Deciding that Dad was not a threat, Raffi turned his attention to Walker, locking his wary, police-dog eyes on the boy. It took him only a moment to realise that Walker was different. Raffi's ear's pricked up, his head tilted to one side – questioning.

Walker gave him a tiny nod, too small for the adults to notice.

He dropped to his knees and offered his hands for Raffi to smell, before burying them in the dog's thick, furry neck.

'He's gorgeous!' Walker said, stroking Raffi's long, soft, pointed ears. Raffi thumped his tail on the mat and made whimpering noises, before rolling over to have his tummy scratched.

'A fine police dog you are!' Krish laughed. 'I've never seen anybody make him do that before.'

'Walker has a bit of a way with dogs,' Dad said.

Krish nodded. 'So it would appear.'

As Walker rose to his feet, Raffi leaned against him.

'Have I done something wrong?' Walker asked.

'Goodness, no!' Krish chuckled. 'I've come with good news. We've found your phone.'

Walker's mind raced back to the day he'd lost it: when he'd discovered a horrible puppy farm in the grounds of Foxley Manor. He'd only just started his dog-walking business and he'd been walking Stella, Jenny Little's spaniel, and Thor and Loki, Arlington Wherewithal's two pointers.

Deep in the woods, they'd found the illegal puppy farm Arlington Wherewithal, the millionaire owner of Foxley Manor, had been running in secret.

Walker had been filming all the evidence on his phone when Wherewithal's creepy gamekeeper, Osmo, had caught him snooping around. The phone had fallen from his pocket as he and the dogs had run helter-skelter through the woods to escape. It had been very scary, but it was worth it.

The puppies had been rescued and Wherewithal sent to jail.

Walker realised that Krish was talking to him.

'D.I. Triggs would like you to come to the police station to pick up your phone.' Krish handed Walker a card. 'Here's her number. You can call ahead to arrange the best time.'

Walker turned the card over. A message was written in neat handwriting on the back.

FORCETSHIRE POLICE
HQ Buildings - Forcet - 3NY

Kayleigh Triggs
Detective Inspector

k.t.triggs@pol.forcestshire.ok   Mob: 077009004900100

*I have some questions I think you may
be able to help me answer.*

What did that mean? Walker wondered. Had his secret been found out?

At the same time, at Foxley Manor, Jazzaminta Wherewithal dumped her shopping bag and a pink straw basket on the huge kitchen table. She slumped into a chair and sighed for the umpteenth time that day.

The pink basket rustled. A miniature Yorkshire terrier jumped out of it, trotted across the table, tilted its head and looked at her mistress in that impossibly cute way that only little dogs with pink ribbons in their hair can.

Her mistress was so sad these days, Camilla thought. Everything had changed.

Jazzaminta swept the little dog off the table and hugged her tightly. 'At least I still have you, Camilla!' she said, kissing the bow on the top of Camilla's soft, silky head.

Wearily, Jazzaminta got to her feet and filled Camilla's bowl. Thankfully, they had a lifetime's supply of Arlington's Precious Princess Pouches, in both gravy and jelly flavours stacked in the cellar. Arlington, her jailbird husband, owned a dog-food company, so at least feeding Camilla was not a problem.

But everything else was. How could Arlington have been so stupid or so cruel? How could she not have known that he and Osmo had been running a puppy farm just a short walk from where she was sitting now? What else didn't she know about her husband?

She'd been to visit Arlington in prison that afternoon. She'd hardly recognised him. He was no longer the funny, handsome man she'd married. He was different – angry and bitter.

He'd left her rattling around their huge house alone. Mrs Stryke, her housekeeper, had disappeared when Osmo ran away. There was hardly any money left in her bank account. She was tired, confused and angry.

Jazzaminta had no one left, except Camilla, her horse, Apollo, and the guard dogs, Thor and Loki, out in the stable yard. They were Arlington's dogs. She tried not to forget them, but she felt so wretched that she sometimes did.

She took a cup of tea into the sitting room and collapsed onto the huge, over-stuffed sofa.

Camilla followed, jumped up and licked her face, breathing Precious Princess Pouch breath all over her, then nestled down on her lap. She was only little, but she would do anything to try and help her mistress get back to being her old, happy self.

Stella heard the gate click. She ran to the sofa and leapt onto the windowsill. Walker was here! The boy gave her a wave as he ran up the path.

Stella jumped down, spun round three times on the carpet, picked up her lead in the hall, and skidded across the shiny kitchen floor. She sat up like a good dog should, with the lead ready in her mouth, waiting for Walker to open the back door.

'You just love that boy, don't you, Stella?' Jenny Little chuckled, as she broke an egg into a bowl.

Walker's mother was allergic to dog hair, so he wasn't allowed a dog of his own. Jenny Little was getting old and couldn't walk very far. So now, every day after school, Walker came to Jenny's house to take Stella out for some exercise in Foxley Fields.

'I'm baking a Victoria sponge cake,' Jenny said. 'There'll be a slice ready for you when you get back.'

Jenny's cakes were awesome. She won the best cake prize at the village show every year. Not only did

Walker get cake, he also got paid for running about and having fun with Stella. Walker loved Stella so much he would have happily paid for the privilege!

At the bottom of Jenny's beautiful garden, a gate took them through a strip of woods, before opening out into Foxley Fields. This was their special place. They could stop pretending once they were through the gate.

Walker had a secret: something that was too difficult to explain; something no one would believe, anyway. Walker could talk to dogs, and dogs could talk to him!

Stella had been the first dog to recognise his special talent and speak to him, right here in Foxley Fields.

'I've got to go to the police station,' said Walker.

Stella looked surprised. 'Have you done something wrong? They're not going to take you away, are they?'

'I don't think so.' Walker furrowed his eyebrows. 'They found my phone. Remember I lost it when we found the puppy farm? I don't know why they can't just give it back. A detective says she wants to ask me some questions. We're going to the police station when Dad gets back from work.'

10

'I really thought we were going to get caught that day!' Stella looked anxious as she remembered those poor puppies. She and Walker had rescued them, with the help of Thor and Loki and the neighbourhood dogs.

'I miss Thor and Loki,' she said. 'They were such fun!'

'I miss them too,' Walker said, wistfully. 'I hope they're all right.'

'Maybe we could sneak up and…?'

'Not a good idea. Mrs Wherewithal probably wouldn't be pleased to see us,' Walker said. 'But it would be nice to see them again.'

Walker fitted a tennis ball into a throwing stick and launched it high across Foxley Fields. Stella leapt into action, racing up the hill after it. She never took her eyes of the ball and snatched it out of the air after one bounce.

'Well caught!' Walker called. He watched her trot back with the ball. A huge feeling of love swelled up inside him. Stella was more than a dog – she was his best friend. He could tell her anything and she would understand.

Nearby, in the grounds of Foxley Manor, shadows skulked through the woods. A startled wren exploded out of the undergrowth; its ear-piercing alarm call incredibly loud for such a small bird.

A Jack Russell terrier growled.

'Shush!'

The dog obeyed its master, but stayed alert, every muscle tense, looking for trouble, itching for a fight.

The man wore camouflage clothes, like a hunter. No one could see him, hidden in the brambles. Like a birdwatcher scanning the landscape for a rare species, he stared through a pair of binoculars. But he wasn't looking for birds.

The dog growled again, low and eager. It had caught sight of another dog. A silly little dog with a pink bow on its head. And there were the other two, in their fancy kennel. Gun dogs! They thought they were so special – so high and mighty!

'There she is!' the man muttered under his breath. 'Looks like she's all alone too!'

Quietly, the man and his dog slipped away

through the undergrowth to the lane where their van was parked.

'She's coming,' Camilla yapped, running excitedly back and forth in the stable yard.

Thor and Loki paced up and down in their kennel, straining to see Jazzaminta as she emerged from the back door of Foxley Manor. They were hungry!

The supply of Arlington's Chumpkin Chunks in the tack room had run out, so Jazzaminta had brought a couple of packs of Arlington's Precious Princess Pouches with her.

Amidst all the riding equipment in the tack room – saddles, reins and halters – she found Thor and Loki's bowls and emptied out the pouches. She shoved the bowls into their kennel and went off to feed and water Apollo, her handsome grey gelding.

Thor and Loki stared at their bowls.

'What is this?' Thor was indignant. Tiny pellets of something that looked like meat floated in puddles of clear, straw-coloured jelly at the bottom of their bowls.

'They look like tadpoles!' Loki hesitated. 'What is it?'

Thor and Loki had been Arlington Wherewithal's pride and joy. But with Arlington in jail, and Osmo vanished, they were looking thin and unloved.

Camilla poked her nose through the chain-link wall of the kennel.

'They're Arlington's Precious Princess Pouches,' she explained. 'They're delicious!'

'But we're not princesses!' Thor growled. 'We need proper food! And we need to run around and get some exercise. We're going stir crazy in here!'

'Just try them,' Camilla sighed.

Loki sniffed his bowl and gave a tentative lick. 'It tastes alright!' he reassured his brother.

Jazzaminta returned, carrying a net full of hay, as Thor and Loki wolfed down their food in one gulp. She sighed. She knew she wasn't caring for the animals properly. Maybe she'd take them all out for a run tomorrow – if she didn't feel too tired.

'What are we going to do?' she wailed.

'If only Walker was here. He'd sort things out for us,' Loki mused.

Thor nodded in silent agreement. Camilla didn't know Walker but, from what Thor and Loki had told her, she thought that maybe the boy could help them. Perhaps he was the only one who could?

15

A surly, crop-haired, young man lurked near the takeaway sandwiches in the village shop. He looked extremely suspicious. Mr Bonus, the owner, watched him.

Sometimes Mr Bonus had a bad feeling about people who came into his shop. Sometimes they looked like they were up to no good, like they might want to rob him.

He's a BAD MAN! Mr Bonus thought to himself.

Mr Bonus felt under the counter for the reassuring shape of the alarm button. His daughter, Anje, was back from school, refilling the coffee machine in the far corner. He flicked his head towards the back door. Anje followed his glance and understood. She closed the lid of the machine and quietly walked to the back of the shop.

Dad had practised this routine with her. With her heart hammering, she bolted the door into the house behind her, made sure the security cameras were working and got her phone out, ready to call for help if there was trouble.

The young man's hood hid his face in deep shadow. He dumped two cans of coke, a cheese and tomato sandwich, a ham and pickle sandwich, two bags of salt and vinegar crisps, a sausage roll and two chocolate bars on the counter. A scorpion tattoo crawled out from the cuff of his sleeve.

Calmly, Mr Bonus rang up the till and said how much it all came to. The youth pulled some notes out of his front pocket and tossed one onto the counter.

Mr Bonus gave him his change and breathed a sigh of relief as the customer left without ever saying a word.

Anje opened the door a crack.

'Is OK,' he reassured her, in his warm Latvian accent. 'But he's up to something,' Mr Bonus growled. The hooded figure sauntered past the window. 'He's up to no good, Anje! I know these things!'

 An old white van was parked next to the shop's side gate. Boss, Anje's dog who guarded the shop, growled through the railings as the hooded youth climbed into the passenger seat.

The driver, a bald, pale, pudgy, greasy man, wore a camouflage jacket, trousers and matching cap. With his aviator sunglasses and wiry, ginger beard, his face was almost invisible. He unwrapped the sausage roll and fed it to the hungry Jack Russell that lay curled up by his feet.

The man in the hoodie took a bite out of his sandwich and looked at Boss through the window. He swigged a mouthful of coke and, baring his teeth, snarled at the dog. Then he choked as the bubbles went up his nose.

Boss could sniff a bad man from miles away, and this was a BAD MAN! Given the chance, Boss would like to catch him and sink his teeth into his baggy tracksuit bottoms!

Detective Inspector Kayleigh Triggs had the palest blue eyes – almost like a husky, Walker thought. Her left pupil was stained with a small patch of pale, sparkling, golden brown.

It was as hard not to stare at her and equally difficult to keep eye-contact with her. Walker felt as if she could see right inside him, like she knew all his secrets, every little naughty thing he had ever done. What was it about the police that made you feel so guilty?

Krish sat next to her with a pen and pad, ready to take notes.

D.I. Triggs reached into a drawer and brought out a plastic evidence bag. She slid it across the table towards Walker. 'I believe this is yours.' She smiled, not blinking.

The bag contained a phone. The case was unmistakeable. It was covered in a paw-print pattern and the protective glass screen was cracked in the shape of a palm tree.

'Thanks!' he said. 'I never thought I'd see this again.'

'Do you know where we found it?' D.I. Triggs asked.

'No?' Walker could feel the blood rushing to his cheeks as he turned a bright shade of crimson.

'We have ways of cracking passwords on phones.' D.I. Triggs smiled again. 'That's how we knew it was yours.'

Walker squirmed in his seat.

'We found it in the woods near Foxley Manor …
near that awful puppy farm. You'll remember it
from the news a few months ago? Do you know
anything about that?'

Walker couldn't say anything. His mouth had
gone as dry as the Sahara Desert. His throat
tightened and his face got even hotter.

'There is an interesting video of the puppy farm
on your phone,' D.I. Triggs said. 'It seems you
discovered the scene of the crime before we did.'

D.I. Triggs had an unnerving way of leaving
long, unblinking silences. Did she think he had
something to do with the puppy farm? Did she
think he was the kind of cruel and heartless
person who could mistreat poor, defenceless
puppies?

Walker's dad cleared his throat, 'You surely don't
think Walker was involved in that, do you?' he said,
defiantly.

D.I. Triggs said nothing. She left Dad's question
hanging in the air for what seemed like forever. She
turned back to Walker and focussed her intense
gaze upon him.

'I– I– I…' Walker stammered. 'I found the

puppy farm. We … I thought I heard a dog in distress and went to help. I couldn't believe what we … I found. Arlington Wherewithal is, like, rich and famous. I didn't think anyone would believe me, so I filmed it to prove it. Osmo, the gamekeeper, heard me. I only just managed to escape, but I lost my phone in the woods. He had a shotgun, you know!'

Walker stumbled over his words. He felt panic rising in his chest.

Dad looked surprised. 'You never said anything! You should have told us!'

'You wouldn't have believed me!' Walker sighed. 'Arlington Wherewithal is … well, I was a bit scared of him. He's very … bossy?'

Dad raised his eyebrows and said nothing.

'I don't suppose you've seen Osmo recently?' D.I. Triggs asked.

Walker felt tongue-tied and confused. 'N-n-no!' he stammered.

'Mr Osmo is wanted for questioning,' D.I. Triggs continued. 'If you do know where he is, or happen to see him, you will let me know, won't you?'

Was that a question or an order?

24

'I've put my number onto your phone, so you have my direct line. It's on speed dial … number one … easy to remember!'

'Y-y-yes! Of course. Thanks.'

Walker had no idea where Osmo was. He'd never liked the man, or his dog, Bolt, and would be happy if he never saw either of them again.

D.I. Triggs consulted her notes.

'Do you remember the night we caught Arlington Wherewithal? All the dogs in Foxley escaped from their owners and ran crazily through the woods, leading us to the puppy farm. Do you know anything about that?'

If there was a brighter shade of red than beetroot, that's the shade Walker turned now. He couldn't possibly explain what happened that night, how all the dogs in the village had come with him to rescue the puppies and reveal Arlington Wherewithal for the cruel bully he was.

He couldn't tell them that he could actually talk to dogs. They'd think he was crazy.

D.I. Triggs narrowed her eyes. 'Constable Malik and I have watched your video quite a few times, haven't we, Constable?'

Krish nodded. A knowing smile played across his lips.

D.I. Triggs leaned forward, resting her chin on her linked fingers. 'We've watched that video again and again and … do you know, it almost looks like you were talking to those dogs?'

Walker felt pinned in a corner. It was getting hard to breathe.

'And it almost looks like the dogs are talking back to you!' D.I. Triggs raised her eyebrows.

Dad broke the silence. 'Ha! Walker has a bit of a way with dogs. Everyone says so. Is that all? Can Walker have his phone back?'

The spell was broken. 'Of course!' D.I. Triggs smiled, as she removed the phone from the evidence bag, and handed it to Walker.

'Would you like to see Raffi?' Krish asked. 'He's in the kennels, out in the yard.'

Relief! The interrogation was over. 'Yes, please!' Walker laughed.

 D.I. Triggs watched the CCTV camera that covered the police station yard.

Krish led Walker over to the kennels and let Raffi out. The dog was overjoyed to see Walker, who knelt down and let Raffi lick his face.

Krish looked up into the camera. He faced the palms of his hands out in an expression that said, 'See what I mean?'

D.I. Triggs nodded. She went back to her desk and carried on filling out a report. But she stored the memory away. She would remember Walker.

 Anje was in the yard at the back of the shop with Boss, having a cup of tea. Her heart was still racing. The shop was their home and for a moment it had seemed in danger. But Boss could always make her feel better and braver.

27

Boss was glad to see her. His job was to protect the shop and protect Anje from BAD MEN, like the ones in that van.

'It's Saturday tomorrow,' she said.

He didn't understand a word she said, not like he understood Walker. But he knew what she meant when she waggled the pepperoni packet!

Anje carefully tore open the packet and squeezed the thin, spicy sausage out half way. 'Dad says we can go out with Walker and Stella tomorrow.'

Boss understood the words 'Walker' and 'Stella'. They were friends but, right now, he was more interested in the brown, spicy meat. He sat and waited for the command.

'Snip!' said Anje.

Boss leapt forward and snipped three centimetres off the pepperoni stick. He chomped it three times to get the full flavour, and swallowed it down.

They did it again, until there was just a stump left.

'Hup!' She tossed the last piece into the air. With a snap, Boss caught it and gulped it down.

Anje laughed. 'Back to work!' It was early Friday evening and homework could wait. Toilet rolls needed to be stacked on the shelves. There were always more toilet rolls to be stacked! What did the residents of Foxley do with them all?

Boss went back to work, pacing up and down, doing his job. Protecting, guarding, waiting for the chance to catch the BAD MEN, like he'd caught that Arlington Wherewithal. He'd so enjoyed sinking his teeth into that BAD MAN'S round, fat bottom!

Arlington Wherewithal lay on the narrow bunk bed in his cell. He was reading an article about online business opportunities in a magazine. The door slammed open.

'Visitor for you!' the prison guard announced. Doors clanged shut and keys turned in locks as Arlington followed the guard through endless, dark, echoing corridors to the visitor's room.

Crispin Lightfoot, Arlington's lawyer and business manager, was waiting for him.

They chatted for a while, discussing whether they could get Arlington's jail-time shortened. When Crispin began talking about money, Arlington's eyes narrowed into a suspicious frown. He folded his arms.

Crispin leaned forward, lowering his voice and nervously flicking his eyes left and right, in case anyone was listening. 'If you could let me know the passwords to your secret bank accounts,' he whispered, 'then I could let Jazz have some cash and sort out your other businesses.'

Arlington said nothing. He stood up and, without looking at the other man again, walked to the door.

31

'Arlington!' Crispin shouted. 'If you don't tell me, someone else will find them.'

Arlington just waited for the guard to lead him back to his grey, lonely cell.

'I bet I can throw further than you!' Anje taunted. 'See that yellow gorse bush? I bet I can throw further than that!'

'Betcha can't!'

Walker laughed, handing her the ball launcher.

Anje took a graceful run up. The ball flew high and far, bouncing just the other side of the bush. Stella and Boss raced after it. Though Boss was bigger, Stella was faster and more agile. She scooped the ball up from the ground as it rolled away towards the long grass at the top of the hill.

'Go, team girls!' Anje laughed.

'My turn,' Walker said defiantly, as Stella returned the ball. The two dogs sat and watched him, eagerly waiting for him to make his move.

Walker took a run up, tripped on a clump of grass, and launched the ball. It went high. It went far. But not far enough. Plomp! The ball landed in the middle of the prickly gorse bush.

Stella and Boss screeched to a halt by the bush and stared forlornly into it. Their body language expressed total disappointment in Walker.

Then Stella saw a rabbit!

'No! Stella! Come back!'

Stella could not resist chasing rabbits. Rabbits were made for chasing and Stella was made for chasing rabbits.

The rabbit headed straight towards the woods. Stella crashed through the trees. Boss followed close behind.

Behind the screen of trees, a raucous cacophony of barking started up, merging with the angry shouts of a woman and the whinnying of a horse, its reins jingling and hooves stamping the soft, leafy ground. Walker's heart thudded.

He ducked under the low-lying branches of the oak trees.

Stella, Boss, Thor and Loki were all bouncing around, joyously barking greetings at one another. Apollo fretted and whinnied. Jazzaminta held Apollo's reins tight, working to keep the huge beast under control. Camilla leaned out of a pink basket tied to the saddle, yapping as loud as she could, just to be part of the noise.

'Can you control your dogs, please?' Jazzaminta thundered.

Anje ran up and joined him.

Walker raised his voice. 'Hello, boys!' he called out.

Thor and Loki stopped dead and stared at him. When they realised who it was, they raced over, knocking him flat to the ground. The two pointers were besides themselves, snuffling Walker's ears and thumping their tails. They were overjoyed to see him again.

'It's good to see you too!' Walker laughed, as Loki slapped a great, wet lick across his cheek.

Walker stood and gave the dogs a commanding look. Immediately, they sat down, panting and gazing up at him adoringly.

Anje watched all the goings on, amazed at the way Walker was just so … what? Just so doggy, like he really understood them.

Jazzaminta settled Apollo. Camilla yapped the last bark, just so everyone knew that she was in charge!

'You're the boy that used to exercise Thor and Loki for my husband, aren't you?'

Walker nodded. 'Yes, miss.'

Jazzaminta thought for a moment, then seemed to make her mind up. 'You wouldn't look after them again, would you? They seem to like you and it would be such a help to me.'

'I'd love to,' Walker smiled, ruffling the dogs' heads.

'Good! Can you come to the Manor tomorrow, say 11 o'clock?'

Walker nodded again. 'Yes, miss.'

'Excellent! I'll see you then.' Jazzaminta almost smiled, as she urged Apollo on, down the path, at a brisk trot.

'Yes, miss?' Anje jeered as they wandered back to the shop. 'Yes, miss. No, miss. Three bags full, miss. It's Saturday. We're not at school!' she laughed.

Walker's cheeks flushed. 'Well, I don't know what to call her. I mean, she is a bit like a bossy teacher, isn't she?'

A white van was parked outside the church, close to the wicket gate that led them into the High Street. Boss growled as they walked past it. Anje only heard the growl; Walker heard what Boss was saying – 'BAD MEN!'

Walker sneaked a look. Two men were slumped in the front seats. One was drinking from a coke can while the other played with his phone. They both wore peaked caps pulled down over their eyes. The late afternoon sun glanced off the windscreen, making it difficult to see them properly. Were they BAD MEN? Boss was usually right. What were they up to?

Sunday morning broke – a crisp, sunny autumn day. Walker picked Stella up from Jenny's and they walked from the bottom of her garden, up to Foxley Manor.

The path crossed a quiet, single-track lane that ran up to an old, deserted barn where teenagers would often hang out. A white van was parked further up the lane. It was almost hidden by the overhanging branches.

'That looks like Boss's BAD MAN van,' Stella said nervously.

They crossed quickly and were soon heading up the drive to the huge entrance porch of Foxley Manor.

There were sleeping bags and blow-up beds in the back of the van. Boss's 'Bad Men' were fast asleep inside. One dreamed he was in an Xbox game, being chased by zombies. He had that dream a lot. The other dreamed of hunting rabbits and foxes … and nosey parkers…!

Bolt, the Jack Russell, slept on the front seat. He heard voices. One ear pricked up. Yes, definitely voices. He yawned, opened his eyes and sat up just enough to see over the dashboard.

It was that boy and that fancy spaniel, Stella. Spaniels always thought they were so clever. It was thanks to those two that he had to live in this van, moving around all the time. If he had the slightest chance, he'd show them what he thought of them!

The sign on the big, old doorbell said, 'Pull'. Walker pulled it.

Somewhere in the distance, a tiny bell tinkled, then he heard Camilla yapping and skittering on the stone floor behind the door.

A key turned and Jazzaminta Wherewithal opened the door. She looked tired. Camilla danced excitedly, bouncing forwards to sniff and check if these were friends or enemies. She decided they were friends and quietened down.

'Oh good! You came. I'm in the office, follow me.'

'Yes, miss. Mrs Wherewithal. Is it OK to bring in Stella? She's very well behaved.'

'No problem,' said Jazzaminta, scuffing down the hallway in her slippers.

Walker followed her into the office. It was pretty untidy. Books, folders and papers were stacked everywhere. Dog-show rosettes were pinned on the walls, alongside photos of Arlington shaking hands with all sorts of famous people – even the Queen!

'I don't suppose you know anything about

computers?' Jazzaminta asked, flopping down in front of a laptop. 'I'm OK sending emails and playing games on my tablet – oh, and buying stuff too, of course – but anything else and I'm lost.'

'I know a bit,' said Walker. 'What's the problem?'

'You met my husband, didn't you? So you know what happened to him? You know he's in prison, right?'

Walker lowered his eyes and nodded. Walker had helped to put him there!

'He's a multi-millionaire, you know? But he's left me completely broke. All he's said is that the key to all his money is in this office. I've searched high and low and I've not found a key anywhere, so I think it must be something on his laptop, like a clue or something?'

'I could look for you, if you like?'

'Can you do that?'

'Yes, miss.'

'The trouble is that I can't trust anyone.'

She looked at the boy in front of her. He was kneeling down, tickling Camilla under the chin. Camilla didn't let anyone do that! Camilla closed her eyes in a state of bliss. Surely, Walker wasn't any kind of threat?

'Can I trust you?' she asked.

'Well, yes!' Walker had no intention of tricking Jazzaminta, but now that she'd asked, he was beginning to feel a bit unsure, the same way D.I. Triggs had made him feel. Oh no! Was he blushing again? Keeping secrets was such a burden!

Jazzaminta let Walker sit in the executive leather swivel chair. Stella lay down underneath. He showed Jazzaminta how to search the hard drive.

Everything looked very standard and boring. There were no games, just folders with names that related to Arlington's businesses or Foxley Manor.

As Walker searched, expertly clicking the mouse, Camilla jumped from Jazzaminta's lap to his. Walker absent-mindedly scratched Camilla behind the ears as he checked through all the main folders.

'Well! That is the darndest thing!' Jazzaminta declared. 'Camilla's never sat on anyone else's lap before.'

'Yes, miss.'

'Please stop calling me miss! It makes me sound like a school teacher. Everyone calls me Jazz.'

'Yes, miss,' said Walker. 'I mean, Jazz, miss.' It didn't feel right calling her Jazz.

'Oh! What's that?'

Walker pointed at an app, hidden inside the accounts folder. The image was a dark design – a pair of ravens.

43

'It's an app called Odin,' Walker explained. 'Shall I open it?'

'Odin?' Jazz whispered. 'I've heard Arlington mention Odin. Something to do with the accounts. Yes, go on,' she said excitedly. 'Open it!'

Walker clicked, and a new window sprang to life.

Across the top of the screen, two ravens sat like bookends on either side of the word, ODIN. The words:

Easy, Secure Asset Management

were written underneath. Below that, a cursor blinked in a box, waiting for a password to be entered.

'You brilliant boy!' Jazz gasped. 'This must be it! All I need now is the password. I hope it's something easy like...' She sucked her teeth, stared up at the ceiling and laughed. 'I know!'

Jazz typed in some numbers. The screen cleared, then reappeared with extra red writing:

Password not recognised.

'That would have been too easy,' she muttered, furrowing her pencil-thin eyebrows.

'What about a birthday?' Walker suggested. 'People often use birthdays as passwords.'

'Great idea! Arlington's got a terrible memory. He'd need an easy password.'

Jazz entered Arlington's birthday.

Password not recognised.

Still no luck.

'He might have used my birthday!' Jazz said. 'Though he did forget it once!'

This time the message was longer.

Password not recognised.

You have had three attempts in the last 24 hours.

You have one more attempt.

Entering an incorrect password will result in extreme app deletion.

The app will reset in 24 hours.

'I think that means you only have three goes a day,' said Walker. 'If you try four time and get it wrong, you'll never get another chance. The app will be deleted. Forever. We shouldn't risk another go.'

After a minute, in tiny type under the message, it read:

Password Hint?

Walker clicked the link.

The words:

Neck Pointer

appeared. Walker threw Jazz a questioning look. She frowned, pursed her lips and shook her head. 'That means nothing to me at all,' she sighed.

Walker looked around. 'You said the key lies in the office. Have you looked in the drawers?'

Jazz rolled her eyes and pulled open a drawer. 'He was so untidy!'

The drawer was a jumble of all kinds of stuff:

- Pens, pencils, a ruler and three bits of old eraser
- four pounds and sixty-three pence in loose change (plus an American quarter and an old German five pfennig piece)
- a packet of paracetamol
- a half-finished pack of Werther's Originals that made Walker's mouth water
- Three pairs of scissors (nail, paper and general purpose)
- a giant glue stick
- a handy pocket-sized pack of tissues
- some kind of microchip reader that seemed to be used to check dog and cat registrations
- three old Nokia phones and two chargers
- lots of fluff
- an antique pocket calculator
- exhibitor badges from a dog show
- some receipts
- a packet of plasters
- two rolls of Scotch Tape
- and a Post-it note dispenser.

No keys!

Sliding the drawer closed, Jazz buried her face in her hands. 'What am I going to do?' she wailed.

Walker didn't know what else to suggest.

'Shall I go and see to Thor and Loki?' he asked.

'Yes … thanks for your help. Do you know the way?'

Jazz waved her hand in the direction of the kitchen and the back door. Her bottom lip trembled. Walker thought she might cry. He quietly tiptoed out of the room, followed by Stella and Camilla.

Hidden in the brambles, the man with the binoculars saw Walker emerge from the back of the house with the spaniel and that ridiculous Yorkie.

Thor and Loki were besides themselves when the boy opened the kennel door and let them out.

Watching with the man, bored and cold, Bolt the Jack Russell growled when he saw Camilla dancing around Walker in the stable yard. Stupid creature, he thought.

Through the binoculars, the man watched Walker pick Camilla up and carry her over to the door at the end of the stables. If he didn't know better, he'd say that Walker was holding a conversation with the stupid little dog as he pointed towards an old wooden bench.

The boy reached under it and pulled out a key.

The man caught his breath. How did Walker find it? No one could ever have guessed that. It was a secret hiding place. It was like he knew!

The boy unlocked the door and quickly emerged with cans of dog meat. How did this boy know they were there? The storeroom was his territory – or it used to be.

Once the dogs were fed and watered, the little group headed across the lawns to the lake and the woods beyond. But not before Walker had tidied up and locked the storeroom door.

The man watched Walker carefully add the key to a keyring, which he put safely back in his pocket.

'Damn!' the man cursed. 'We need a new plan!'

'Proper food and a proper walk!' Loki and Thor cheered, racing towards the lake, their elegant name tags jingling on their collars. 'Since Arlington went, she hardly ever lets us out,' Loki complained.

'And she often forgets to feed us!' Thor added.

'Thank Camilla!' Walker laughed. 'She knew where the key to the storeroom was, and she knew there was food inside. There are boxes and boxes of Chumpkin Chunks in there, so you are not going to starve any time soon.'

Thor and Loki raced Stella to the little jetty. 'Wahay!' Thor yelped, as the three dogs launched themselves into the lake, barking with the joy of their reunion and new-found freedom.

'There is no way I'm going in there!' Camilla announced. Thor climbed out of the water, grinning wickedly. He shook himself vigorously, spraying a rainbow of cold, dirty lake water all over Camilla!

'Waah!' Camilla retreated as fast as her little legs would go.

'Well, thank you very much!' she griped. 'I don't know when I'll ever get another shampoo. Jazz forgets everything these days. Fridays are always my shampoo days. It's Sunday today and she's totally forgotten.'

'I suppose she has a lot on her mind,' Walker mused.

Mrs Wherewithal – Jazz – was no longer the haughty lady of the manor that she used to be. Walker had never actually spoken to her before, but he'd seen her out and about in the village, and always thought she was a bit scary.

Now he felt sorry for her. Her world had come crashing down around her. She even looked smaller than she used to. She'd always looked so smart and well-dressed with her hair piled on top of her head. Now she moped around in jeans and a sweatshirt, her hair all tangled like she'd just got out of bed.

'Anyway,' Walker brightened up. 'I'm here to look after you now. Everything is going to be A-a-a-a-l r-r-r-ight!!'

They had to cross the little lane that led to the old barn as they followed the footpath around the estate.

An engine started close by. Gears crashed, and a white van accelerated towards them.

'Woah!'

Walker pulled the dogs back into the long grass and weeds at the side of the track.

A Jack Russell jumped up to the driver's window, jammed his nose through the open gap and barked a jeering insult at them.

The driver turned his face towards them. His ginger beard split into a thin, insincere grin.

'OSMO!' Walker's blood turned cold.

'BOLT!' All four dogs, barked in unison.

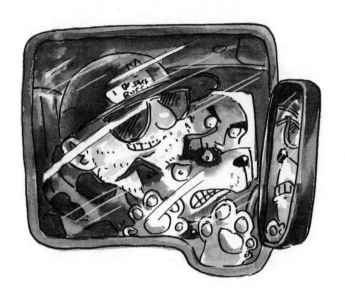

'There you are, you little minx!' Jazz scooped Camilla up into her arms and was just about to give her a kiss when she stopped and wrinkled her nose. 'Pooh! You need a bath!' she complained.

'Camilla came with us and got a bit wet near the lake,' Walker laughed, tickling Camilla under the chin. 'She had a great time, though, and she walked all the way round. She's very tired!'

'Did you walk all the way on your ownsey-wownsey?' Jazz cooed in a baby voice, as she rubbed noses with Camilla.

'We saw Osmo.'

Jazz's head snapped round. 'That man! I never liked him. I can't think why Arlington ever hired him. Tell me, where was he? What was he doing?'

She fired questions at him and Walker told her everything he'd already reported to D.I. Triggs on the phone. He thought it best not to mention that he'd spoken to the police.

Walker hosed and dried the dogs. Jazz hadn't cleaned them out in a while, so there were quite a few dried-up parcels of poo lying around in the kennel. It wasn't the most pleasant job, but Thor and Loki didn't deserve to live in such conditions. Walker scooped them all up on a shovel and threw the hard little sausages into the bushes.

'I'm off now!' Walker called though the kitchen door. 'Mum said to be back for Sunday lunch at one o'clock.'

'That sounds so nice.' Jazz pulled a sad, tired smile as she sat down, buttered a crispbread and cut a slice of mouldy-looking cheese.

'I'll come back tomorrow, after school,' Walker reassured her.

'Bless you,' she said, getting up to lock the door securely behind him.

D.I. Triggs found Constable Malik feeding Raffi in the police station yard.

'I just had a call from young Walker,' she said.

'Oh yes?' Krish stood up and rolled his shoulders. 'And…?'

'He's just seen Osmo, with another man, in a white van. He said they were driving quite fast, so they're probably far away by now. He said that Osmo definitely knew that Walker had clocked him.'

'Very interesting,' said Krish, scratching his beard.

Raffi stood to attention, waiting for orders. It sounded like some bad men needed sorting out!

After school, the next day, Walker fetched Stella to go up to the manor and give Thor and Loki some exercise.

'Don't you feel funny going up to the manor?' Jenny asked. 'You know … after all that puppy-farm business?'

'It's not Thor and Loki's fault,' Walker explained. 'They haven't done anything wrong, and someone needs to look after them.'

'I suppose it's too much hard work for that woman to look after them properly…' Jenny's voice trailed off. Anything to do with Arlington Wherewithal made her feel hot and bothered.

'Are you OK?'

'Pass me that bottle, will you?' Jenny gasped. 'It's my angina!'

Jenny sprayed something under her tongue.

'Do you need the doctor?' Walker was worried. Stella put her head in Jenny's lap and whimpered her concern.

Jenny patted Stella's head for reassurance. She closed her eyes for a short while, until her breathing slowed down.

'I'm OK now,' she said at last. 'You're right. It was Arlington who was the bad one. I've really got no reason to get angry about her.'

'I honestly don't think Mrs Wherewithal knew about anything Arlington did. She's angry with him too.'

Jenny smiled. Walker was such an honest, caring boy. 'Go on,' she said. 'Off you go. Those dogs need you.'

 'Is Jenny OK?' Walker asked Stella, as they made their way up to the manor.

Stella nodded. 'Yes, she goes funny like that when she gets excited or upset.'

Jenny's angry words rang in Walker's head. 'So, what do you think of Jazz?' Walker asked Stella,

'Oh, I think she's a nice lady,' Stella said. 'Camilla thinks she's the best thing since Precious Princess Pouches, but she's terribly worried about her. She says she's been so sad since Arlington went to prison.'

Thor and Loki could smell Walker and Stella long before they caught sight of them. They were wild with excitement by the time the pair appeared in the stable yard. 'We haven't had any breakfast,' they complained. 'We haven't seen Jazz all day. Her bedroom curtains are still closed!'

Walker fed and watered them, then took them for a walk through the woods, so they weren't tempted to jump in the lake. He didn't have time to clean them up today!

When they returned, a gleaming red Jaguar XJ was parked in the stable yard. As Walker put the boys back in the kennel, the back door opened, and a man walked out.

Crispin Lightfoot, Arlington's business manager! Walker had never spoken to him, but he'd seen the two men together. There was something creepy about him. Stella growled to let him know that she felt the same way.

'Oh! It's you. The dog boy.' Crispin Lightfoot sneered down his long, thin nose at Walker.

Camilla appeared in the doorway, growling and baring her tiny, needle-sharp teeth.

'Let me know if you have any ideas, Jazz,' Crispin Lightfoot called back to Jazz inside. 'Good day to you!' He mock-saluted Walker as he climbed into his car. The door of the Jaguar clunked behind him. The engine purred and the car slipped quietly down the drive.

Walker tapped on the open back door. 'She's in the office,' said Camilla.

Jazz sat in the swivel chair. She was slumped across the desk, her head in her hands.

'Are you OK?' Walker asked. She had dark rings under her bleary eyes.

'I didn't sleep well last night,' she explained. 'It's all this worry!'

'Was Mr Lightfoot any help?' Walker gestured towards the back door.

'That man! I trust him less than Arlington. He's Arlington's lawyer, but I think he's a crook. He says he wants to help me find Arlington's money, but I think he wants to get his own hands on it! He was snooping around. He knows the key is in this room, whatever the key turns out to be.'

Walker wasn't sure what to say.

Jazz's face softened. 'I'm sorry,' she smiled. 'You don't need burdening with my problems, but all my friends have deserted me since Arlington went to jail. I've no one else to talk to.'

'It's OK,' said Walker. 'I just came to tell you that I've fed the boys and I took them for a walk. I wondered if you would like me to come up early and feed them before school? I can come on my bike, it won't take me very long.'

'Oh! Bless you. You are such a sweet boy. That would be marvellous!'

Walker gave the boys their breakfast and fed and walked them with Stella after school every day that week. By Saturday morning, when the alarm clock rang, he felt very tired. At least there was not such a rush today, as he didn't have to get to school.

'I hope Mrs Wherewithal is paying you well for all this work?' Dad asked, shovelling another mouthful of Crunchy Nut cornflakes into his mouth.

Walker pulled a face.

'She is paying you?' Mum frowned.

'Well, yes … I think so. It's just she hasn't actually said how much, but Thor and Loki need me and…'

Mum shook her head. 'Dogs!' She rolled her eyes. 'What are we going to do with you?'

When Walker went to get Stella, Jenny's curtains were all closed. Stella was waiting for him behind the kitchen door.

'Jenny's not feeling well!' She whimpered. 'She's still in bed.'

'Is she OK?' Walker frowned.

'Could you come and see?'

Walker pulled the keyring out of his pocket. Jenny had let him have a back-door key, just in case.

The keyring had popped out of a cracker last Christmas. The key fob was a shiny, metal dog bone. What were the chances of him getting that in a cracker?

He crept up the stairs, calling softly, 'Jenny … are you OK?'

He'd not been upstairs in Jenny's house before. He guessed which was the bedroom and went in.

'Jenny?'

Slowly, Jenny rolled over and opened her eyes. 'I had a terrible night,' she said. 'I've a pain in my hip,' she explained. 'I've run out of ibuprofen. Could you go to the shop and get me some?'

'Hi Walker! You're early!' Anje was putting price labels on tins of tuna.

'Jenny's not well,' he explained. 'She's asked me to get her some ibuprofen.'

64

Mr Bonus folded his arms. 'I should not be selling painkillers to young person.'

'Oh, please, Mr Bonus,' Walker begged. 'Mrs Little's hip is really aching and she hasn't slept all night.'

As well as being Anje's dad, Mr Bonus was Walker's business mentor. He'd advised him on how to set up his dog-walking business and how to advertise for customers.

He reached behind him to where they kept a few medicines, and put a packet on the counter for Walker. 'Because it's you, I make exception.'

'I'll see you later,' Walker called across the shop to Anje. 'I'll go and feed Thor and Loki, and ask

Jazz if they can come with us to Foxley Fields. I'm sure she'll say yes. I'll be back about half past ten.'

'See ya later!' Anje waved.

She picked up a tin of beans, changed the price on her label gun and began sticking the price labels on the tins in the brand-new box she had just opened. People ate so many beans! She was always putting prices on tins of beans!

Boss sat by the gate at the side of the shop. He stood up when he saw Walker.

'Hey, Walker!' he called through the wrought-iron bars. 'The BAD MEN are back. I saw that white van go past early this morning. They are up to no good!'

'Thanks for the tip-off,' Walker said. 'I'll keep my eyes peeled and let the police know if I see them too.'

'I hope Jenny is all right,' said Walker. He'd given her the ibuprofen and made her a cup of tea before taking Stella up to the manor.

Stella was thinking mostly about rabbits. There always might be a rabbit around the corner. She couldn't smell one, but there were lots of smells left by other dogs that were equally interesting.

Phew! Google, the Bedlington Terrier from number 36, had been along the path this morning already, and left a mighty stink behind him!

Once they were off the path and in the grounds of the manor, Walker let Stella off the lead.

'Meet you at the kennels!' she barked, running off across the wide sweep of lawn that led to the back of the house.

But she was back very soon.

Something was wrong. Walker could tell by the way Stella ran, all hunched-up and tense-looking, nervous.

'What's up?' he whispered, sensing that they shouldn't draw attention to themselves.

'It's the van we saw Osmo driving,' she said breathlessly. 'The van Boss didn't like. The one he said had BAD MEN in it ... and Bolt! I was down wind and smelled him. I don't think he saw me.'

'Let's sneak round the side of the house and peek in the windows. That'll be the office window over there.'

Walker pointed to the corner of the building, where the Virginia creeper was growing up the walls in fantastic shades of red and yellow.

Walker clipped Stella onto the lead. He felt braver being connected to her, and Stella felt safer attached to him.

They crept along the side of the house, keeping their heads down, popping up to look into the ground-floor windows. Nothing seemed unusual or out of place.

The windows were ancient – little diamond panes held together with strips of lead. They didn't stop any sound like double or triple-glazing would. Walker heard voices from the room at the end. The office. They crept along the wall, keeping their heads down.

Something in the tone of the voices made him nervous.

'I'm calling D.I. Triggs,' Walker whispered, pulling his phone from his pocket and pressing the speed-dial number that D.I. Triggs had programmed into the memory.

Before he could even raise the phone to his ear, he felt a terrible pain in his neck, like the pincers of a giant beetle grabbing hold of him from behind. His blood ran cold.

 'I'll have that!' A bony hand, decorated with a vicious-looking scorpion tattoo, grabbed the phone out of Walker's hand and stuffed it into his back pocket.

The man held Walker's neck in a vice-like grip. Walker was pulled up into a crouching position. His shoulders were scrunched up in agony.

Stella started barking like a lunatic.

The man lashed out with his foot, side-swiping Stella in the ribs. She squealed. The man grabbed her lead, making Stella choke.

'You two little nosey parkers are coming with me!' He spoke with a nasty, raspy voice that made Walker even more scared.

The man dragged them round the house and through the back door.

Bolt was beside himself in the van, out in the stable yard. His snout stuck out of the window that had been left open a crack for him. His teeth were bared, snarling, baying for blood.

Thor and Loki joined in the din. They were helpless, locked in their kennel. Barking was all they could do. Something really bad was happening in the house and they were stuck outside!

The man pushed Walker down the corridor. Stella tried to dig her claws into the stone floor, but the man just dragged her along behind him, choking her more. Then he shoved both of them through the office doorway.

It was such a relief to be free of the pincers on his neck. It took Walker a moment to take in the situation. He saw Stella was in a state of shock, cowering as the man tied her lead to the door handle.

The room was empty – totally empty! No desk or laptop or executive swivel chair. No photographs on the walls, no filing cabinets … nothing! Everything that had been in there when he'd first visited last Sunday, even the carpet, had gone!

Sitting in a kitchen chair by the window, head held high and defiant, Jazz glared at a short, stout man with a ginger beard and a greasy cap, which was embroidered with a picture of a dog and the slogan 'I ♥ Jack Russells'.

Osmo!

The man behind Walker spoke. 'Look what I found snooping around outside!'

'Let him go this instant!' Jazz ordered. 'He's just a child.'

Walker smiled, despite everything. This was the old Jazz. All her sadness and worry had disappeared. She was Lady of the Manor once more, and she was not going to take any nonsense from these two scallywags!

Osmo stared at Walker. His pale-blue, piggy eyes crinkled with malign pleasure. 'I might have known you'd turn up, you sneaky little kid.'

'It's all right. I got his phone,' the other man growled, holding it up and waggling it, just out of Walker's reach. He put the phone safely in his back pocket.

'Tape him up,' Osmo ordered.

Walker realised that Jazz's hands were bound together behind her back.

'You can't do that to a child!' Jazz insisted, as she watched the horrible, younger man jerk Walker's arms behind his back.

There was a loud, angry rip of duct tape, as he tore off a length and wrapped it round Walker's wrists.

Osmo sneered. 'Get the other dog!' he ordered.

The other man left the room, then returned, holding Camilla up by the scruff of her neck.

Camilla wriggled and yapped and snarled bravely, trying to bite the hands that held her tight.

'Now,' said Osmo, with a deep and theatrical sigh. 'Let's try again. We know the key was in this room, so where is it now? What have you done with all the stuff?'

Boss was pacing up and down in the back yard when Anje came out of the shop to get him ready for their Saturday morning walk with Walker and Stella.

In the distance, he could hear two dogs barking, warning of danger. But the sound was so far away, he could only sense the urgency of the barking, not the meaning.

'What's the matter, boy?' Anje laughed. 'Are you so desperate for a walk?' She looked at her watch. It was a quarter to eleven. Walker was already late. Anje frowned. 'Walker should be here by now'.

Boss wasn't listening. Something was wrong. There were BAD MEN out there and they were not far away. It was his job to catch BAD MEN!

'For the last time, where is all the stuff? An office doesn't just empty itself by magic. Where's it all gone?'

Osmo was losing his temper.

A fleck of spit flew out of his mouth at Jazz. She pulled her head away.

When he'd been Arlington's gamekeeper, Osmo had been in the office many times, collecting wages or discussing shooting-party plans with Arlington. He knew exactly what should be in the room.

He had been secretly watching Jazz's movements over the last week. He'd planned to sneak into his old gamekeeper's storeroom and get the spare back door key. Then he could sneak into the house when she was out, copy the laptop hard drive, and creep out again without anyone noticing.

But this stupid boy had pocketed the keys and spoiled his nice and simple plan.

Osmo had had to go back to Crispin Lightfoot for new instructions.

Osmo and Scorpio – yes, that really was the other man's name – had returned to the village early in the morning. They'd parked down the drive and waited. Osmo understood dogs. He had parked down wind, so Thor and Loki couldn't smell them and bark a warning.

Jazz came out to see to Apollo. As she went back into the house for breakfast, they'd made their move.

As bold as brass, they'd screeched into the yard, slammed on the brakes, jumped out and bundled a shocked and surprised Jazz into the house, down to the office. All they had to do was nab the laptop and go. Except, the laptop wasn't there. There was nothing there at all!

'Oh dear!' Osmo had said. 'You've gone and made this really difficult.'

'Go and pickle your stupid, fat head,' Jazz snarled.

Walker was amazed. She was so brave. He looked at Stella for reassurance.

Stella was staring at her lead – it was tied to the door handle. She gave him a whine, telling him that it would be quite easy to undo – if she had the chance – if the horrible men could be distracted. She could feel a breeze from the back door. The man hadn't closed it behind them, so escape was possible!

Osmo pulled a penknife from his pocket. Walker

could see it was a Swiss Army knife. He'd had always wanted one, but his mum said he was too young.

Osmo pulled out a tiny pair of scissors from the side of the knife with his fingernails. He snipped and snapped in the air.

'Let's start with that stupid little bow!'

Scorpio held Camilla tight.

She bared her teeth, snarling and growling at him, but she was so tiny, there was nothing she could do with Scorpio holding her so tightly.

Osmo pulled up the tuft of hair that tied up today's fresh pink ribbon, and clipped it off in one smooth chop! He waved it about between his index finger and thumb, then tossed it casually into the fireplace.

The room fell silent. Walker and the dogs turned to Jazz. How would she react?

She blinked slowly and took a deep breath. 'All right,' she sighed. 'I'll tell you. If you promise not to hurt anyone.' Her shoulders slumped in defeat.

Stella and poor Camilla were stunned into silence.

'I had everything boxed up yesterday, and put into a storage unit,' Jazz explained. 'After Crispin Lightfoot came here, sneaking around, trying to find the key to Arlington's missing millions, I thought it was the safest thing to do.'

'It was the stupidest thing to do,' Osmo growled.

At that moment, a voice called out from Scorpio's back pocket. 'Walker?'

Scorpio pulled the phone out of his pocket and stared at it with a stupefied look of amazement. A woman's voice spoke from the tiny speaker. 'Walker? Are you all right?'

Camilla felt Scorpio loosen his grip. Like a streak of lightning, she swung her head round and snapped, sinking her tiny teeth into Scorpio's hand. The man howled with pain, letting go of Camilla and the phone.

Camilla ran to protect her mistress. The phone spun and arced through the air, the voice still calling, 'Walker? Is that you?'

It was the distraction Stella had needed. She slipped her lead off the door handle, leapt in the air, caught the phone clean in her mouth and ran for the back door.

'Camilla! Go with her!' Walker bellowed. 'Go to Boss and Anje! Get help!'

Camilla paused and looked at her mistress. There was nothing she could do to help here. She sped off down the corridor and out of the house.

Osmo dived after her, but he was too slow. He crashed to the floor, his weight making it a hard, uncomfortable landing. It hurt a lot.

'My hand!' Scorpio wailed. 'That dog bit my hand!'

'Oh, shut up and stick it under the cold tap!' Osmo growled. He was really angry now.

 Out in the stable yard, Bolt ran up and down the seats in the front of the van, hurling himself at the doors, barking, barking, barking! Stella raced past, but there was nothing he could do. The doors were locked and the windows only left open a crack for fresh air.

Thor and Loki were barking too, leaping up at the chain-link walls of the kennel run. 'What's happening?' Thor yelped.

'Where's Walker? Where's Stella going?' Loki howled.

'Can't stop!' Camilla answered, as she skidded past the kennels. 'We'll be back soon!' She raced after Stella.

Across the lawns they ran together, down to the path along the back of the High Street.

'What's happening?' Boss called over the fence, as he heard them coming.

'The BAD MEN have got Walker!' Camilla barked. Boss began howling.

Anje, in the back yard of the shop, tried to calm the big, powerful dog. But Boss's blood was up. There were BAD MEN on the loose!

Stella and Camilla squeezed under the gate at the bottom of Jenny's garden, raced through the vegetable patch, over the wall, into the High Street, and zoomed up to the side gate of the shop. Boss was waiting for them. Every sinew in his body was tense, twitching, ready to go and catch the BAD MEN.

'Stella! What are you doing here? Where's Walker?' Anje was worried now. 'What have you got there?'

Stella dropped the phone through the wrought-iron gate.

Anje recognised it immediately. No one else would have that naff, doggy-print phone case. 'It's Walker's phone! Where is he? What's the matter?'

'Hello?' said the voice on the phone. 'Who's there?'

Anje put the phone to her ear. 'Hello? I'm Anje, Walker's friend.'

'This is D.I. Triggs from the police. I think your friend is in trouble. Can you tell me exactly where you are and what's going on?'

Boss dragged Anje through the shop. His loud barking frightened some of the customers. A toddler in a pushchair began to cry.

'Hey!' Mr Bonus called out. 'No dog in shop!'

'Sorry, Dad!' Anje called over the din. 'Gotta go.' She waved the phone at him. 'Walker's in trouble! It's an emergency!'

She opened the door and Boss hauled her out into the street, where Stella and Camilla were waiting, barking for them to hurry up.

'Sorry, ladies and gentlemen!' Mr Bonus announced. 'My daughter!' He threw his hands up in the air, as if that explained everything. 'Hah! Everything OK now. Everyone do nice shopping.'

He offered a Chupa Chups to the wailing toddler. The crying stopped immediately and the tears turned into a smile. 'Is sugar-free,' he reassured the child's mother.

 After Walker had pressed number one on his phone's speed dial, D.I. Triggs had heard everything.

It had taken her a while to work out what was going on

and to realise that Walker was in trouble and call out his name.

She'd heard the commotion and the great escape, and Stella panting all the way from the manor to the shop. Then she'd finally got to speak to Anje, who was as confused and concerned as she was.

'Don't do anything stupid!' D.I. Triggs yelled down the phone. 'I'm sending a patrol car right now.'

But Anje had already closed the call and was on her way to help her friend.

Constable Malik was driving past the shop. D.I. Triggs had called him on the radio and told him to get to Foxley as fast as possible.

Walker! The boy had a knack for getting involved in adventures!

There was something special about him though. Walker didn't just 'have a way with dogs' as everyone said. Constable Malik thought that he was good with dogs, but Walker was in a different league. He knew there were people called Dog Listeners and Dog Whisperers, who could handle dogs and sort out their behavioural problems. He'd replayed and rewatched video footage from Walker's phone many times. It really did look as if the boy could actually talk to dogs!

Just then, a girl ran out of the shop. She was being dragged along by a barking German shepherd that looked just like Raffi. Raffi heard the commotion and joined in, turning agitated circles inside his crate in the back of the van.

What was going on? Constable Malik's police senses were tingling.

The girl and the dog were following two other dogs, a spaniel and a Yorkie. They raced down the road and disappeared through a gate into a garden.

Wasn't that the dog Walker looked after? Something was going on, and it needed investigating now!

 'Everything from the office is in a security lock-up unit on the industrial estate,' Jazz explained.

'How do you get into it?' Osmo panted. He was still winded from his fall.

'I have to sign in at the desk. There's some sort of camera-recognition thing they use. And there's a hefty padlock on the unit door,' said Jazz.

'Can anyone else sign in?'

'I'd have to write a letter and you'd have to show a driving licence or passport to prove who you are.' Jazz hoped the security details might put them off.

'Can you take people with you? Or do you have to go in alone?'

Jazz paused, her eyes flickering. Walker could tell she wasn't sure what to tell them.

Osmo also saw that she was stalling. He nodded at Scorpio, who grabbed Walker's neck in that vice-like pincer grip again. His neck was already bruised from the last time and now it really hurt.

'Owwww! Let go!' he shouted.

'Let him go!' Jazz snapped, angrily. 'He's just a boy!'

Scorpio bared his teeth in a semblance of a smile. 'He's a nosey little tyke!' But he did loosen his grip.

'I can take up to three other people with me to carry stuff,' Jazz explained quickly. 'I just have to sign in myself and say how many there are with me.' She glanced at Walker as if she had a plan.

Osmo pointed at Scorpio, Walker and then himself. 'One, two, three! Perfect. So, where's the key to the padlock?'

'In the kitchen drawer, to the left of the Aga.'

Scorpio came back holding the key triumphantly. A laminated label hung from it, with the storage company's name and logo printed on it, as well as a QR code.

Osmo examined it. 'Unit 24b, Foxley Box Storage Company,' he read aloud. 'I know where this is. Let's go!'

They pulled Jazz and Walker to their feet, marched them to the van in the yard and bundled them into the back.

'Right,' said Osmo, putting his hands on his hips and deciding on a plan. 'This is what we are going to do...'

Constable Malik was attaching Raffi's lead when D.I. Triggs's car squealed to a halt behind his canine patrol van.

'What's up?' he asked. as the D.I. got out of the car.

'Walker called me on the phone,' she said. 'Except he didn't say anything. It was an open line. It sounds like he's been taken hostage. It was all a bit confused. I think they're holding a woman, too. Probably Arlington Wherewithal's wife. They sound nasty.'

'What's the plan?' Constable Malik asked.

'It seems a dog escaped with the phone. Eventually I spoke to a girl called Anje, a friend of Walker's. I told her to stay where she was, but she said she had to help him.'

In the distance they heard dogs barking.

'She went that way,' said Constable Malik, nodding towards the gate of Jenny Little's house. 'Come on, Raffi. Follow the scent and lead the way!'

D.I. Triggs called the police control centre. 'We need back-up in Foxley. We are making our way to Foxley Manor on foot now.'

'Keep up!' Camilla barked. She might have been the smallest, but she was plucky, leading the pack along the path and up towards the manor.

Anje tried to keep up with Boss, who was barking like crazy, telling Camilla all about BAD MEN and what he'd do to them when he caught them.

As they entered the stable yard, Thor and Loki made a terrible din, hurling themselves at the kennel run's wire walls. Apollo leaned out of the stable door, staring wildly, neighing loudly and stamping his hooves.

Camilla and Stella just glimpsed Walker and Jazz, wriggling in the back of the white van. Stella would never forget Walker's terrified look as Osmo slammed the doors shut. He was being taken … who knew where?

'Let's get out of here!' Osmo growled at Scorpio. The engine thrashed into life.

As Anje turned, panting, trying to work out what was happening, the van manoeuvred backwards and forwards with a crashing of gears. A cloud of blue exhaust filled the yard.

Osmo wound down his window and curled his lips in a grimace. Bolt jumped up beside him, barking insults at Boss.

That was the last straw. These were BAD MEN!
Boss saw red and lost all self-control.

He lurched forward with all his strength, ripping
the lead out of Anje's hand, almost pulling her
shoulder out of its socket. Boss set off after the van.
It was full of BAD MEN and a BAD DOG!

'Ow! Boss!' Anje screamed as she fell onto the
hard, cobbled floor of the stable yard.

 Constable Malik was helping
Raffi over the stile that blocked
the path to the manor, when
they heard the girl's pained cry.
D.I. Triggs gave him a worried
look and leapt over the stile.
They ran, picking up their pace, crossing the lawns
that swept up to the manor house.

'I'm getting a bad feeling!' she called.

'Me too!' Constable Malik gasped.

 Stella rushed to help the girl, who was lying on the ground, holding her shoulder. She butted Anje's forehead, trying to make her get up and open the kennel door to release Thor and Loki. Why couldn't she understand? Thor and Loki's fresh legs were needed to take up the chase after Walker.

She ran backwards and forwards to the kennel. Come on! she thought. Come and open the kennel door!

'Can you undo the hook?' Thor asked Stella. He was desperate to escape the kennel and race after the van. He had never liked Osmo, even if he had once fed him every day. Walker needed him and Loki now. They needed to get out.

Stella leapt at the hook. It was quite loose and jangled as she nudged it with her nose. She should be able to … nearly! Try again … and again! On the fifth attempt, the hook popped out of the eye it was lodged in.

'Now the handle,' Thor encouraged. He and Loki waited on the other side of the door, as Stella reached up a paw and did her best to pull the handle downwards. She reached as far as she could. The handle moved a bit, the latch clicked half way open – but not enough. Stella could see a thin gap of daylight. Try again?

Before she recovered her balance, Thor yelled, 'Go!' The two dogs pounded across the kennel run and hurled themselves against the door. The lock gave way under their weight and burst open, propelling Stella across the yard.

'Sorry,' said Loki. 'Are you all right?'

Stella was more worried about Walker. She didn't care if she was hurt or not.

'I'm OK,' she said. 'How's Anje?'

The four dogs gathered around the girl, deciding just how injured she was and whether they could leave her. Stella sniffed Anje's shoulder. They could hear Boss barking in the distance, as he chased the van down the drive.

Humans give off different smells. Stella could sense Anje's injury and the level of pain she was feeling. It wasn't too bad. There was also a faint, distracting whiff of pepperoni … mmm! Delicious!

'She's hurt,' Stella told the others. 'But not badly. She'll be OK. Come on, let's go!'

'I'm so sorry you're mixed up in all this,' Jazz said.

She and Walker struggled to lean up against the sides of the van. As the vehicle careered down the twisty drive, they were thrown against each other.

'Are they going to hurt us?' Walker asked. His throat was dry. He was trying to be brave, but he was on the verge of crying.

'I don't think so.' Jazz smiled reassuringly. 'Osmo's a thug, but he's not stupid. They've kidnapped us, so they're already in big trouble. He won't want to make it worse for himself.'

'I saw my friend, Anje, as they were closing the doors,' Walker said. 'Stella and Camilla had fetched her and her dog, Boss. She'll call the police. They'll save us.'

'I hope so,' Jazz sighed. 'I hope they save us before Osmo nabs Arlington's missing millions!'

Anje saw the police trio run into the yard. The dogs around her looked up. Suddenly, as if someone had given a signal, all four took off down the drive.

'Are you Anje?' D.I. Triggs asked. 'Are you OK? Has someone hurt you?'

'Boss!' Anje winced as she tried to sit up.

'Whose boss?' Constable Malik asked, concern affecting his voice. 'What did he do to you?'

'Boss is my dog!' Anje groaned. 'Boss pulled the lead out of my hand. Don't worry about me. They got Walker! They took him in a white van. And

Mrs Wherewithal too. All the dogs have gone after them.'

'Hello, Control?' D.I. Triggs spoke into her phone. 'Is that back-up on the way? Good. Tell them to look out for a white van being chased by a pack of dogs ... I know,' she sighed. 'It sounds ridiculous! We also have an injured girl.'

'Funny how packs of dogs are involved when Walker gets mixed up with serious crime!' D.I. Triggs muttered from the side of her mouth.

Anje showed them Walker's phone, trying to think how to explain what had happened when she wasn't sure herself.

D.I. Triggs recognised it. 'Walker's phone,' she said. 'That's a shame, we could have tracked him if he still had it.'

Constable Malik gave her a beaming smile. 'Raffi has a locator chip on his harness. If we let him follow the dogs, they might lead us to the van. I can track him on an app on my phone.'

Raffi was straining at the leash, desperate to get going. He had a job to do.

D.I. Triggs thought for a moment. 'It's worth a try.'
The policeman unhooked his lead and spoke
gently in his ear. 'Go find Walker!' Raffi was off like
the wind, down the drive following the baying
pack. Anje watched him go.

'The van turned left, out of the gate,' said Thor. 'We can cut through the woods. Come on!'

They'd caught up with Boss now. The pack crashed into the undergrowth and through the thick woodland.

'Oh! A puddle,' Stella panted. 'I'm desperate for a drink!' She began lapping up the brown water as if she'd never had a drink before in her life. Camilla joined her.

'I can't keep up with you,' the tiny dog sighed. 'I'm too little. My legs are too short and I'm exhausted.'

'You've been a real hero!' said Stella. 'Go back and look after Anje. She needs someone with her. Now, who's this?'

A German shepherd wearing a smart police harness bounded up to them.

'Which way did they go?' he demanded.

'Follow me!' said Stella, heading off after the others. 'See you later,' she called to Camilla.

'Take care!' said the little dog. She turned and trotted a lonely path back to the manor house.

The road skirted round the side of the woods. The van was having to go all the way round the trees, while the dogs could cross straight through.

As they broke through the edge of the woods, the van zoomed past them on the road below. The van's tyres squealed as it took a sudden turn onto the busy dual-carriageway that skirted the village.

'We'll never catch them now!' Loki groaned.

'I'll get 'em,' Boss growled.

Raffi raced in front, before anyone could move, and barked an order.

'Police. Stop right there!' His commanding tone made them all sit obediently.

Raffi had experienced many chases and dangerous situations in his police career and knew what to do. 'We need to keep calm, assess the situation and come up with a plan,' he said, calmly.

Stella sighed. It was so reassuring to have a professional leading the pack.

'Look! The van is turning at the traffic lights,' said Loki. He'd not taken his keen eyes off the van for a moment. Loki stood tall and erect, his nose pointing in the direction of the industrial estate across the dual-carriageway. His front right paw was raised and his tail was raised, horizontal and quivering. At this height at the top of the hill, they could see a long way into the distance.

They watched the van pull up outside a large industrial unit. It parked alongside other cars and rental vans. Saturday was always a busy day at the lock-up, as people came to store, move or collect their stuff.

A minute later, Osmo and Scorpio climbed out and opened the back doors of the van.

'Right!' said Raffi. 'There is no way we can cross the carriageway. It's far too dangerous and we may well cause a road-traffic collision.'

That thought had never crossed the minds of the other dogs, who were all ready to go careering across all four lanes of the carriageway, never mind the traffic!

'Look, there's a bridge over there.' Raffi nodded away from the industrial estate. 'It's a long way round, but we should be able to cross the road in safety.'

Boss could only think about the BAD MEN. He could see them hauling Walker and Mrs Wherewithal out of the back of the van. With his

keen, sensitive ears, he thought he heard Walker
cry out, as the men ripped the tape off his hands.

'Grrrr! Let's go!'

 'Ow!' The tape tore Walker's
skin, as Scorpio ripped it off his
hands. But it was such a relief
to be unbound and able to
move his arms again.

'Right!' said Osmo. 'This is
what we are going to do…'

Osmo took a deep breath, smoothing down his
clothes and tidying his hair. Walker guessed he
didn't want to look too suspicious.

'Her ladyship here will sign us in as helpers,
come to move something heavy from her unit.
We will all smile and be polite. Then we will go
to the unit, unlock the door, find the laptop and
leave together. We will then release you two,
somewhere you can catch a bus back home.
Understand?'

Scorpio, Jazz and Walker all nodded.

'Let's make this nice and easy,' he continued. 'Any funny business or any heroics, and you will both regret it… Still understand?'

Jazz and Walker nodded again.

'Right. Smile, and let's go!'

'Raffi's heading towards town.' Constable Malik aligned the map on his phone. A red dot blinked alongside the line of the dual-carriageway.

The locator chip on Raffi's harness sent a satellite position code to the app every three seconds. It was accurate to within two metres. 'Take the right turning here,' Malik instructed the driver.

They'd been picked up from the manor by a patrol car, leaving a police constable to guard the house and report anything suspicious.

Anje was feeling a little better, now the shock was wearing off. Camilla had trotted back and sat next to her, trying to look cute and helpful, though that wasn't easy without her ribbon and a chunk of fur missing from the top of her head.

They sat in the back of the police car, Anje hugging Camilla with her good arm. Constable Malik decided Anje should stay with them in case she had to catch Boss and get him under control.

'He's been trained to catch BAD MEN,' Anje explained. 'But he'll do anything I tell him.'

It was very exciting driving in a police car, but what was her dad going to say when she got home!

'What the…?' Constable Malik pointed at a footbridge, just before they went under it.

Five dogs raced over it. D.I. Triggs saw from the back window that the pack turned left on the other side, going in the opposite direction.

Raffi's red location dot changed direction on the map and headed away from town.

'Turn around!' Constable Malik told the driver.

D.I. Triggs' phone was still connected to the control room. 'Order all units to Foxley Industrial Estate,' she said. Then she put her phone in her pocket and prepared herself for action.

 'Hello, Mrs Wherewithal. Back already? Did you forget something?'

'Hello, George,' Jazz beamed at the man behind the desk at the Foxley Box Storage Company. He pointed to an iPad that was fixed to the wall.

'If you'd like to sign in?' he smiled.

'We've just come to pick up a few bits.'

Walker thought she was being incredibly brave and cool. As long as she was, he could be too.

Jazz waved the QR code that was printed on the key fob at the iPad camera. The iPad scanned her face and a green smiley appeared on the screen.

'Now, if your helpers could just sign in, too?' George suggested.

Jazz glanced round, almost smiling. Was this her plan? Walker wondered. She hadn't mentioned this when she'd said what would happen. Would Osmo give up if he had to sign in?

Osmo hesitated a moment, but then he shrugged. He typed a name into the iPad – Justin Beeber – and smiled for the camera. He typed the names David Jason for Scorpio and Wally Wherewithal for Walker. George printed out stickers for them to wear in the building.

'Justin Beeber!' George exclaimed. 'Like the pop star?'

'It's spelled different,' Osmo smirked.

'Right, chaps!' Jazz said brightly, acting brilliantly, though Walker could see fear in her eyes. 'Come this way.'

George pressed the security button and the big doors opened with a hiss, letting them into the warehouse.

It was harshly lit by cold LED lights inside. Corridors led off the main aisle. Each storage unit was padlocked. One or two doors were open and the voices of the owners drifted out from inside their units.

People used these storage units for many reasons. Some had no room left in their houses to store stuff so, instead of sorting it and getting rid of it, they started filling up a unit as well. Some stored things for their businesses or work, while others used it to keep things safe while they were living abroad. Some even stored stuff to hide it from prying eyes!

'Here we are,' said Jazz, unlocking the enormous padlock and opening the doors. The roof was made of thick steel mesh, which let in the light from above, but the unit had lights inside too.

Scorpio pushed Walker inside and closed the doors behind them. It was a tight squeeze with all four of them.

Walker looked for a way to escape and save Jazz and himself. But Osmo or Scorpio were watching him all the time. What would their captors do once they had what they had come for?

 'This way!' Raffi called. The others didn't need telling, They'd picked up the scent and were racing past parked-up vehicles and rubbish dumpsters.

'There's the van!' said Stella.

Raffi sniffed the ground and looked up at the warehouse. 'They're in that building!' he snapped.

Five dogs raced towards the entrance. The automatic doors were set to sense adult human beings, so as not to let children or passing animals in. How could they get inside?

Just then, the doors whooshed open to let a customer out. This was their chance. The pack raced into the reception area.

'What the…!' George slid out of his chair onto the floor behind his counter. Five dogs were leaping at the doors to the inner warehouse, barking and howling to be let in. He ducked down and phoned 999.

'Hello? I need the police. This is the Foxley Box Storage Company. We are under attack! A pack of dogs are going crazy in here!'

The police radio crackled into life.

'All units in the Foxley area, make your way to Foxley Box Storage Company on the industrial estate,' the controller announced. 'They're having problems with a pack of wild dogs.'

'Boss!' Anje gasped.

'Turn right at the lights,' D.I. Triggs ordered. 'And turn on the blues and twos!'

The blue lights flashed. The two-tone siren blared. Their hearts started pumping with the insistent sound. The traffic around them ground to a halt, letting them swerve through the red light, and onto the industrial estate.

 The warehouse was an echoey place. Five dogs barking at the top of their voices filled the place easily.

'What's going on?' Scorpio sounded spooked.

Osmo looked worried. 'Where's the laptop?' he demanded.

Jazz found the box and undid the parcel tape. The laptop sat on a pile of paperwork.

Osmo grabbed it. 'Right, let's go!' he hissed.

A wailing police siren joined the barking, followed soon after by two more.

'Cops!' Osmo spat.

'There's the van,' said D.I. Triggs, pointing at the warehouse. The car screeched to a halt by the entrance. 'Anje, stay here.' She looked at Constable Malik. 'You ready, Krish?'

He nodded and pointed to the red dot on his phone. 'Raffi's in the warehouse!' he said. 'Let's check out the van first. The hostages might still be inside.'

Bolt leapt up and down at the window of the van, adding to the din, barking and snarling at the two police officers as they approached.

Stealthily, with their batons at the ready, they slipped round to the back and pulled open the doors. The van was empty save for a couple of dirty sleeping bags on blow-up mattresses and a canvas toolkit.

George popped his head above the desk as they ran into the building.

'Th-thank God you're here!' he said. He nodded towards the dogs. 'They just burst in through the doors and went berserk! I hope they haven't got rabies or anything!'

As he spoke, Camilla raced in and joined the other dogs, adding her high-pitched bark to the deafening chorus.

'Raffi! Sit!' Constable Malik ordered.

Raffi was surprised to see his master. He obeyed immediately, and passed the order on to the others. All five dogs, stopped barking and sat down. They turned their heads towards Constable Malik and waited for further instructions, tongues hanging out, panting to get their breath back and dribbling all over the floor.

D.I. Triggs turned to George, who was still cowering behind the desk. 'Can you let us inside, please, sir?'

George pressed the button and the doors swung open.

D.I. Triggs, Constable Malik, five dogs and a back-up unit of six coppers warily entered the warehouse.

'This is the police!' D.I. Triggs bellowed. 'Come out and give yourselves up! The place is surrounded.'

Seven terrified, and totally innocent, unit owners appeared in the aisle with their hands up. D.I.Triggs motioned them forward and told them to report to a police officer outside. She called through the door to the reception desk. 'Seven … is that everyone?'

'Al-l-l-most,' George stammered. 'Just four left inside. Mrs Wherewithal and her three helpers. Two men and a boy. I think he's her son.'

 Walker heard the dogs and then the police sirens. An incredible feeling of relief washed over him. Surely this was over now?

But Osmo pushed them all back. The units had locking handles inside, so you could be secure while sorting out your secret and precious things. Osmo jerked the handle and locked them in. He pulled out his phone and made a call.

'Ello? Crispin? We've got a problem!' He turned away from the others and spoke in hushed whispers before turning back to the other three.

'If we're going to jail for this,' he smiled ominously, 'we might as well crack the code now.'

 He put the laptop on a pile of paper files, opened it and pressed the start button.

'OK, Crispin,' he spoke into the phone. 'I've got it logged

into the guest WiFi. I've opened the app and it says Odin at the top. It's asking me for a password.'

Walker and Jazz locked eyes. A look passed over Jazz's face as if to say, 'They're going to steal all Arlington's money. I'll be penniless!'

Osmo typed in a password. 'No, that doesn't work,' he told Crispin.

He typed another, and another.

'Password not recognised,' he whispered to Crispin. 'It says: "You have had three attempts in the last 24 hours. You have one more attempt.

Entering an incorrect password will result in extreme app deletion. The app will reset in 24 hours." We haven't got 24 hours, Crispin!'

Osmo looked at Jazz.

She shrugged her shoulders. 'Don't look at me! I've tried every password I can think of. Arlington never told me anything!'

Would Osmo see the password hint? Would Crispin Lightfoot know what **Neck Pointer** meant?

 In the silence that followed, Walker thought he could hear whispers and the squeak of trainers on the concrete floor outside the unit. He hoped it was the police come to save them.

Crispin's tinny voice echoed out from the phone, giving Osmo final instructions.

'OK,' Osmo said, typing a password for the fourth time. 'You'd better be right or we are in big doggy doo-doo!'

He finished typing and pressed Enter.

'It's doing something!' he said excitedly. 'Well done, Crispin. I think you've done it … Oh! Wait a minute … The screen's flashing red!' he hissed into the phone. 'It says, *final attempt incorrect!*'

The cooling fans in the laptop began to whirr, faster and faster, louder and louder! A thin wisp of smoke curled up through the letters G and H on the keyboard. The wisp grew into a small cloud, then bright flames streamed out of the keypad, engulfing the laptop and setting fire to the paper files underneath.

Osmo looked terrified. 'It's burst into flames!' he yelled at the phone.

Walker was transfixed by the sight. The flames were licking higher and higher as the paper in the files caught fire too. A bitter, acrid stench hit the back of his nose.

Walker realised that Osmo and Scorpio were distracted and he saw his chance.

He rushed to the door, slammed the handles open, grabbed Jazz's arm and pushed her ahead of him into the corridor.

Stella and Camilla raced towards them and leapt into their arms.

'Stella!' Walker cried.

Jazz tucked Camilla under her arm and ran to the police at the end of the corridor.

Walker clutched Stella to his chest. Tears streamed down his face as she licked his face with joy.

He was safe. It was all over!

Choking smoke filled the corridor. The smoke detectors set off loud alarms and flashing lights, which lit up the smoke like a disco. It was chaos!

Scorpio ran past Walker, trying to escape. Raffi

leapt into action. He streaked down the corridor and leapt at the man's arm the way he had been trained to do.

'Get him off me!' Scorpio screamed. 'I give up!'

'Get down on the ground!' Stella barked at Walker. 'The air currents blow fresh air across the floor so you can breathe better.'

But before Walker could drop to his knees, Osmo stumbled out of the unit. Seeing that the police were covering both ends of the corridor, he grabbed hold of Walker, using him as a shield.

'Get back!' he yelled, coughing and spluttering in the smoke. 'Everyone get back, or the boy gets it!'

'Let me go!' Walker shouted. He kicked and struggled and tried to bite Osmo's hand, but the man was incredibly strong.

Stella joined in, biting Osmo's leg.

Osmo kicked her down the corridor. She skidded across the shiny floor, yelping with pain.

Walker struggled even harder. How dare Osmo kick Stella!

He was fighting so hard, Osmo had no time to think about what anyone else was doing – or any of the dogs.

Boss was covering the exit behind Osmo. His blood boiled over. That BAD MAN had hurt his friend, Stella, and now he was hurting Walker.

He fixed his eyes on Osmo's big, fat, round bottom, bared his teeth and charged!

Fifteen minutes later, Walker, Jazz and Anje were huddled in blankets as they watched the fire from behind the police line.

Fire engines filled the parking lot. Firemen ran about directing jets of water at the warehouse, which was engulfed in flames. Thick smoke spilled upwards into the crisp, blue autumn sky. Half the village had come out to watch, and the dual carriageway had ground to a halt, as passing cars slowed to gawp at the scene.

Someone had got them cups of hot chocolate from somewhere. It tasted so good!

'I was so glad to see you, Stella.' Walker buried his head in the fur of her neck. 'And as for you!' Walker gave Boss a big hug. 'You saved my life!'

'It was nothing,' said Boss. 'It's my job – catching BAD MEN!'

'It was a job well done,' said Raffi. 'Not quite the method we are taught in police training, but your style was very effective.'

'Aw! Thank you,' Boss spluttered. 'That means a lot, coming from you.'

Raffi turned to Thor and Loki. 'And you boys were heroes, too.'

They glowed with the praise.

Camilla poked her head out from under Jazz's jacket and coughed.

'And you're a heroine,' said Walker, chucking Camilla under the chin.

Walker and Anje's parents had been fetched by the police.

'Anje! My little baby!' Mr Bonus wept tears. He squeezed his daughter so tight she thought her eyes might pop. 'And Boss! You good boy! You save Anje from the BAD MEN. Good boy! Good boy!' He grabbed Boss in his other arm and squeezed them both as if he'd never let them go.

'Oh, good lord! Walker, are you OK?' Walker's mum was almost hysterical. Her son was wrapped in a blanket, his hair was matted with soot and his face was covered in smoke stains. He looked like an old-fashioned chimney sweep. 'Come on. We need to get you home!'

'What about Stella?' Walker said. 'We'll have to bring her with us. There's no way Jenny can come out here to get her.'

'How are we going to do that?' Mum asked. 'You know I'm allergic to dog hair. She can't go in the car.'

'I can follow you in the patrol car, and bring Walker and Stella with me,' said D.I.Triggs. 'That's the least we can do for our young hero!'

Hero? Walker didn't feel like a hero. He felt like an ordinary boy who had survived a scary adventure. All he wanted to do now was to go home, have a bath and … eat something. He was starving!

Mum was convinced that the village was full of robbers and kidnappers and refused to let him walk the dogs as usual the next day.

By teatime, Walker was pacing up and down, worrying about Stella, Thor and Loki.

D.I. Triggs and another detective had visited and had asked questions most of the day, slowly writing down his official statement about the kidnap, robbery and arson. They had taken forever! But, at last, he'd signed the statement and they'd gone.

Walker eventually convinced his parents that it was quite safe for him and Stella to walk up to the manor, to feed Thor and Loki and take them out for a run.

'Jazz might not have fed them,' he said. 'I need to check they're all right. All the bad guys have been caught and locked up! The dogs saved me!'

'Dogs! Dogs! Dogs!' Mum sighed.

The curtains were still drawn at the manor when Walker and Stella entered the stable yard.

Thor and Loki were thrilled to see them. They wagged their tails like windscreen wipers in a thunderstorm. 'Walker! Stella! Are you OK? That horrible man, Osmo. We never liked him!'

'I'm OK,' Walker reassured them. 'My neck aches and I'm very tired. But it's all over now and I'm much happier being here with you guys. Mum's being a pain, fussing over me all the time.'

'What about you, Stella?' Loki asked. 'He really kicked you hard?'

'I'm fine,' she said. 'I'm a bit bruised, but I'll survive. I was more worried about Jenny. I thought she might have a panic attack when she heard what happened, but she was more concerned about me and Walker.'

The pair of pointers fell silent for a moment, before they said in one voice, 'We haven't had any breakfast yet!'

After he'd fed the boys, Walker was too tired for a long walk, so he settled down on a pile of golden, fallen leaves and watched the dogs chase each other across the lawn. It seemed their adventure was already forgotten. The dogs saw him lean back, staring up into the sky. A breeze swished the tree tops and a shower of leaves dropped to the ground, settling all around him.

They came and lay down next to him. They didn't need to say anything. They sensed that Walker needed a moment of quiet. Thor edged forward until his nose was practically pressing up against Walker's.

Walker looked into Thor's deep, brown, trusting eyes. He stroked the dog's velvet ears between his thumb and forefinger. He took in all the tiny details: Thor's twitching whiskers; the dark brown spots on his white snout; his Chumpkin Chumps' breath; the pinkness of his tongue that lolled out of the side of his mouth; the red stitching on his collar; the chunky buckle and the ornate name tag that hung from it.

Next to the name tag was a small silver tube, about half a centimetre wide and three centimetres long. A line around the centre suggested it would come apart if it was pulled.

'What's that on your collar, Thor? I've never noticed it before.' Walker leaned over and examined the tiny tube. 'There's something engraved on it – writing – it says ... ODIN!'

Walker sat up. 'Neck Pointer!' he said, excitedly. 'You are pointers and your collars are on your necks!'

'Arlington keeps little strips of paper in the tubes,' Thor said casually.

'Let me see.' Walker twisted the tube. It was a close fit, but with a bit of twisting and pulling, the

132

two halves came apart. A roll of paper nestled inside.

Walker's heart began to race as he unrolled the paper and read it. It was a string of numbers, split into groups, with full stops between them. He'd helped Dad set up the new WiFi at home and recognised the pattern.

'I think it's a website address!' Walker was excited now and the dogs sensed it.

'What does it mean?' Stella asked.

'I don't know yet,' Walker said.

Loki had a tube as well. It too had 'ODIN' engraved on it and contained the same roll of paper with the same numbers on it.

'A back-up!' Walker exclaimed. 'What did Arlington do with these bits of paper?'

'He only ever looked at mine the once,' Thor said. 'He did something with his laptop thing, and then he read our chips.'

'Chips?' Walker looked confused. 'What chips?'

'Jazz! Mrs Wherewithal? Are you there?'

Walker pulled the porch doorbell again and again. Eventually, he heard Camilla's claws click on the stone floor on the other side of the door.

Walker peered through the letterbox. 'Camilla! Where's Jazz?'

'She's in her bedroom,' the little dog called up to him. 'She's lying in bed with some old black-and-white movie on the telly. She's fast asleep!'

'Go and get her for me.' Walker's voice was filled with urgency. 'We've got good news!'

Anje sat in the sunshine in the yard behind the shop. Once all the excitement was over, and the fire at the warehouse was under control, her shoulder had really begun to hurt. Her dad squeezing the life out of her hadn't helped either!

An ambulance lady had reckoned nothing was broken, but she'd put her arm into a sling so she could give it the rest it needed. Dad gave her the day off! No putting price stickers on baked beans for her today.

'You were amazing, Boss,' she said. 'You were so brave, catching Osmo like that, and saving Walker too! All you dogs were amazing – even Camilla. She was such a comfort, coming back to be with me when I'd been hurt.'

She didn't want to say it was Boss's fault she'd been hurt, and Boss didn't want to think it either. He'd done what he had to do to protect her from the BAD MEN! That was his job.

Of course, Boss didn't understand a word she said. He was focussed on the last piece of pepperoni.

'Hup!' Anje tossed it in the air. Boss leapt up and snapped it down in one gulp.

The air was crisp and cool, but there was still warmth in the sun. Boss lay down by her side. Anje leaned back against the wall and ran her fingers through his deep, thick fur.

'You know how everyone says how good Walker is with dogs?' Boss looked at her with his big brown eyes, almost as if he really understood. 'Well, sometimes I think...' She smiled to herself. No, that was a crazy idea.

'Walker! What's the matter?' Jazz was in her dressing gown. Her hair hung down in greasy straggles.

'Look!' Walker waved the tiny scrolls of paper at her.

'What are they?' Jazz looked sleepy and confused. She had been up late the evening before, making her official statement to the police. Yesterday's ordeal had taken its toll, however brave she had been at the time.

'They're web addresses!' Walker said excitedly. 'They were hidden in little containers on Thor and Loki's collars. Neck Pointer – like on the pointer's

136

necks! They had ODIN engraved on them. I think I've worked out the password. Can we use your iPad?'

Jazz looked even more confused, but Walker's enthusiasm was beginning to wake her up.

'Type these numbers into the browser,' said Walker, when they'd sat down at the kitchen counter. 'Now press enter.'

'It's not going to set fire to my iPad, is it?' Jazz looked worried.

'The app has been deleted forever. But this isn't an app, it's a website. It should be OK.'

A blue line crawled across the top of the browser as it connected to the website. Two Ravens and the words ODIN – Easy, Secure Asset Management appeared on the screen. Below it, a cursor blinked in a box, waiting for a password.

Jazz's eyes popped wide open. 'Oh, you amazing boy!' She was wide awake and excited now. 'So, what's the password?'

'I don't know, exactly,' said Walker.

Jazz groaned and her shoulder's slumped. 'We're so near to finding Arlington's missing millions and yet so far!'

Walker smiled. 'But I think I know where to look.'

Jazz frowned at the boy. 'What do you mean?'

'Arlington said the key was in the office, right?'

Jazz nodded.

'I think he was telling the truth. Do you remember all the stuff in the desk drawer? All that normal office kind of stuff? One thing seemed to stick out – the chip reader.'

'Chip reader?'

'Thor and Loki have both been chipped. You know? A little microchip they put under the skin on a dog's neck. The chip reader gets the registration number and looks up the details of the dog and the owner if they get lost. I think their chip numbers are the password and the chip reader is the key!'

'You brilliant boy! How on earth did you work that out?'

Walker winked at Thor and Loki, who were skulking in the kitchen doorway.

Jazz sat bolt upright. 'What are you two doing in here? You're not allowed in the house!'

Thor and Loki looked very guilty. They hung their heads, tucked their tails between their legs and went to wait outside on the porch. They'd never been inside the house before. In all the excitement, they'd forgotten they weren't allowed!

'We need a chip reader.' Walker raised a hopeful eyebrow at Jazz. 'Any idea where we can get one?'

Jazz picked up her phone and scrolled though some numbers. 'Polly's a friend of mine,' she said, as she waited for the call to go through. 'She's a vet – and she owes me a favour! '

'Polly!' She raised her voice, as Polly answered her call. Jazz was her old self now: charming, gracious and persuasive.

Jazz and Polly chatted for a bit, before Jazz got to the point, 'Polly, dear … I need a favour!'

'She's going to pop over in an hour,' she said, as she put down the phone. 'I think you should be here too.'

 It took a lot of persuading on the phone. Mum wanted Walker to come home right then. He'd had a big fright and needed rest. But Walker couldn't rest, not while there was unfinished business.

'Mum, Mrs Wherewithal says she really needs me,' Walker pleaded.

'How much is she paying you?' Mum asked. 'You almost live up there! She's the one that got you into all this trouble in the first place!'

Walker looked at Jazz. Jazz still hadn't mentioned anything about paying him. He'd have to ask Mr Bonus for some business advice about that.

Jazz took the phone from him and instantly soothed Mum's fears. 'I really do need Walker's help,' she explained. 'I promise I'll drop him back home as soon as we're done. Your son has been such a help to me. You must be very proud of him.'

 Polly arrived in her Range Rover. 'I've got to get to a sick cow over in Davendon,' she said. 'I'm afraid I can't stay.'

140

That was perfect. Polly ran the chip reader between the shoulders of both the dogs and read out the codes. They were different.

'Could you check under their necks?' Walker asked. Thor had told him that Arlington had got the password from a chip in his neck, not between his shoulder, where registration chips were usually inserted.

Polly frowned. 'We don't put chips there. And dogs don't need two chips.'

Jazz gave her a look that said, Please? Humour the boy!

So Polly put the chip reader under their chins.

'Well, I never!' Polly read out the number from under Thor's neck. Loki has a second chip too, with exactly the same number. 'That is bizarre!' Polly blinked. 'Why would anyone want to…?' Her voice trailed away.

'Back-up!' Walker whispered to himself.

Jazz sighed theatrically. 'That's Arlington for you!'

Polly looked embarrassed at the mention of Arlington and made excuses to go.

As soon Polly's car disappeared round a bend in

the drive, Jazz gave Walker a conspiratorial wink and said, 'Come on!'

The iPad sprang to life on the kitchen counter. The cursor was still blinking, waiting for them to enter the password.

Carefully, Walker read out the numbers and, holding her breath, Jazz typed them in.

She crossed her fingers and said, 'Here goes!' She pressed Enter.

The blue line crept along the top of the browser window again, as the website connected. The window went blank for five seconds.

Then a string of numbers poured onto the screen.

Jazz screamed and hugged Walker. Stella and Camilla barked and chased their tails, as Jazz grabbed Walker's hands and danced him round the room.

'Oh, you clever, clever boy!'

Jazz wiped the tears from her eyes and looked more carefully at the screen.

'Twenty-five million, three hundred and forty-five thousand, eight hundred and ninety-four dollars and sixty-four cents! TWENTY-FIVE

142

MILLION, THREE HUNDRED AND FORTY-FIVE THOUSAND, EIGHT HUNDRED AND NINTY-FOUR DOLLARS AND SIXTY-FOUR CENTS! All these years, Arlington's been hiding this from me. This is a secret bank account in the Cayman Islands that I never knew about! Well, I know now!'

 At school, the headteacher told everyone in assembly how brave Walker had been. All the other kids wanted selfies with a real, live hero. He'd been interviewed by the press and had even been on the local TV news!

After school, an envelope was waiting for him on the door mat.

Going away for a while. Apollo and the dogs are being looked after. See you very soon and thanks for EVERYTHING. P.s I owe you some wages.

143

The envelope was stuffed with twenty-pound notes. Walker counted it out on the kitchen table. 'Five hundred pounds!' he gasped.

'I should think so too!' said Mum. 'After all the danger she put you through.'

D.I. Triggs recommended Walker and Boss for Public Bravery Awards.

Anje and Stella came with them to Police Headquarters, where the chief constable made a speech about the wonderful, brave youth of today, and awarded them medals and certificates.

They all had their pictures taken, shaking the Chief Constable's hand – even the dogs!

Boss and Raffi had their pictures taken with Walker and Constable Malik, in his best uniform.

'Well done, Walker,' D.I. Triggs said, with a little laugh in her voice. 'Next time we have a problem solving a crime, we know where to find you!'

Walker smiled nervously. He wasn't sure if she meant it for real or not!

The weeks went by. Life got back to normal again.

Walker and Anje met up on Saturday mornings, running about on Foxley Fields, throwing tennis balls for Stella and Boss to catch.

Then, one Saturday, Stella caught sight of a rabbit.

'No-o-o-o!' Walker yelled after her. 'Stella! Come back!'

Stella crashed through the trees and into the woods at the top of Foxley Fields. Boss followed close behind.

Behind the screen of trees, a raucous cacophony of barking merged with the laughter of a woman and the unmistakable whinnying of a horse, its reins jingling, its hooves stamping the soft, leafy ground underfoot.

Walker's heart leapt as he recognised the sounds.

'Hello, Walker! Hello, Anje! How are you two?'

Jazz was like a new woman. She sat high on Apollo's back, eyes shining, dressed smartly in riding gear. Camilla popped her head out of her basket. A bright pink bow adorned her head.

145

'Camilla!' Walker frowned. 'Your fur has grown back fast!'

'I took her to the hairdressers with me!' Jazz laughed. 'They gave her hair extensions until her fur grows back! Doesn't she look gorgeous?' Jazz tickled the back of Camilla's neck.

'I'm going away again on Monday,' she smiled. 'I'm going to the Cayman Islands. I have some business to attend to there.' She winked conspiratorially at Walker. 'I may not be coming back.'

'Oh!' Walker was surprised at how sad he felt to hear that news. He and Jazz had been through a lot together. He'd begun to think of her more as a friend than the lady of the manor.

'Do you want me to look after the boys?' Walker said, letting Thor and Loki lick his face.

'Actually, I was going to call by this afternoon and talk to you about that. Thor and Loki are going away to live somewhere else. An old friend of mine runs an estate in Yorkshire. Thor and Loki aren't pets, you know? They're working dogs. They need to be out and about all day.'

Thor and Loki tilted their heads and stared trustingly at Walker.

Walker felt a lump growing in his throat.

'It's going to be great fun,' said Thor enthusiastically.

'We love you very much,' said Loki, 'But we are gun dogs, you know?'

'I'm going to miss you guys,' said Walker, taking a dog in each arm and hugging them.

To anyone watching, it just looked like a boy hugging two dogs.

'You know?' Jazz turned to Anje. 'If I didn't know better, I'd say those dogs understand every word Walker says.'

Anje looked up at her and smiled. 'You know, I've had the exact same thought. And, sometimes, I even think Walker understands every word they say back!'

Walker and all five dogs froze and stared at Jazz and Anje.

'Me? Talk to dogs? Don't be silly! Ha!' Walker laughed, nervously. 'Ha-ha! Ha-ha-ha-ha!'

Loki rolled over first, howling and waving his legs in the air. Thor was next, then Boss, then Stella: all four of them baying like lunatics, wriggling about on their backs. Camilla bounced about in her basket on Apollo's saddle, snuffing and howling as only a tiny Yorkie can.

Apollo stamped and whinnied.

'Oh my goodness!' Anje exclaimed. 'I think they're laughing at us!'

How to draw Walker and Stella

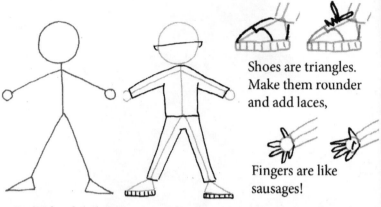

Shoes are triangles. Make them rounder and add laces,

Fingers are like sausages!

Begin by sketching out a stick-person in pencil. Then 'hang' Walk clothes on the frame using ink.

Add quarter circles for ears on the centre-line of his face.

Erase the pencil lines.

Shade Walker in to finish!

Draw Walker's fringe first, then the outline of his hair. Add eyes, nose, mouth, collar and school badge.

Begin drawing Stella by sketching out a stick-dog in pencil.
Then draw her body in ink, by following the lines above.

Draw the outsides of Stella's ears first, then draw the inner
lines. Draw the eyes, nose, tongue and collar.

To draw Stella's paws,
just draw two curving
lines in the 'blob' at the
end of her feet.

Finally, erase the
pencil lines, before
shading or colouring-
in the picture.

If you love drawing
then go to my
website, where you
will find hundreds of
how-to-draw videos
to help, inspire and
maybe help with
homework too!

www.shoorayner.com

Firefly

At Firefly we care very much about the environment and our responsibility to it. Many of our stories involve the natural world, our place in it and what we can all do to help it, and us, survive the challenges of the climate emergency.

Go to our website **www.fireflypress.co.uk** to see some of our great environmental stories.

We are always looking at reducing our impact on the environment, including our carbon footprint and the materials we use, and are taking part in UK-wide publishing initiatives to improve this wherever we can.

Walker and Stella love the fields and parks around their home. Do you have a favourite outside space, maybe a garden, a park, the mountains, or the seashore? Whether it's near home or somewhere you hope to travel to one day, finding out all you can about it will help you protect it, which helps us all.